# THE DAYS OF NO WORRIES

LET'S RELIVE OUR SCHOOL DAYS

SAMEEKSHA JUNEJA

I would love to

Dedicate this book

To my loving

***Parents, Grand Parents***

***& Guru Ji .***

# Contents

# Contents

# Foreword

What life is?

Is it battling for a superior future or partaking in the present?

She got the answer to this question in Robin Sharma's book.

"*Have fun while you are advancing along the path of your goals, purpose, and dreams.*"

And afterward she likewise felt that we have a solitary life and no one of us needs to kick the bucket with dreams, all need to bite the dust with recollections. We continue to hustle the entire day however neglect to zero in on our wellbeing and satisfaction of our desires. We have a solitary life and we need to satisfy our objectives and wishes both.

Then, at that point, she found out about composing this book. Along appreciating with her companions, partaking in her school life, why not gather this multitude of minutes in her book. What's more that would carry a grin to her and others' appearances as well.

She looked upon this and observed no book connected with her theme. Hazard taking and trying different things with new things have forever been in her blood. She chose to gather this multitude of minutes as story-like sonnets with practically no rhyme and in Hinglish language.

Without having the apprehension about the number of deals it would make. She worked upon the execution of her idea with no feelings of dread.

She chose to publish this book within 90 days. She kept three months since she needed to dedicate time to her academics as well. This being her first venture, she really wanted the opportunity to find out with regards to promoting, distributing, and a lot more things.

Yet, attempted to do everything she possibly can without running towards flawlessness because

"*Perfection is the enemy of good*"

-Voltaire

# Preface

This book would take you on a journey of your school life. The most blessed time of our life without any worries. School is very special to a student. It is a place where students from different backgrounds come together to learn. It offers magic in the form of experiments in laboratories, sports in the field, creativity in the art room, and most importantly, it teaches us many social skills. It is so hard to imagine a world without schools.

And the poems of this book would take you on a journey of your school days. The days of asking for one minute from mother to sleep more, those sleepless nights during exams. From all hands in a single lunch box, to eating in-between the classes. Those P.T periods, self parents' signatures, group photos, that silly fights we used to do were just amazing, and still now, the reasons on which we fought bring smile to our face.

Sonnets are written in Hinglish language with practically no rhyme, yet with a ton of feelings. Takes you on that 12-year venture brimming with tomfoolery, learning, and a ton of recollections. These sonnets will assist you with remembering your recollections of your school and companions and would carry a grin to your face.

I accept extraordinarily in gaining and gaining from others' errors as well. I keep on gaining from others' slip-ups. I was having this idea as a main priority and finally, I have composed 3 significant things I learned while composing this book. They would without a doubt show you something.

Happy Reading

# Acknowledgements

I offer my genuine thanks with collapsed hands to Mrs. Navneet Sandhu Brar and Mrs. Geetika Juneja Grover who assisted me with editing this book.

Large on account of my dad(Mr. Gaurav Juneja) who helped me in getting this rich book cover planned, and my mother (Mrs. Neeru Juneja) who has been a consistent help all through and consistently propelled me.

I'm incredibly appreciative to God for giving quality individuals close by

Furthermore

Genuine on account of every one of them.

# 1. School hai kya?

*School hai kya?*
*Ek building hi toh hai,*
*Jisko ham jail samajhte the.*
*Aur jahan apni Zindagi kai 10-12 saal guzaare the.*
*Vacations mai school Jaane ka mann karta tha,*
*Aur school days mai chhutiyan chhate the.*
*Par roj school toh jaana hi pdta tha.*
*Kabhi parents dantt kar bhejhte the,*
*Toh kabhi friends kai liye jaate the.*
*Vaise kahen toh school ki harr cheez hi best thi.*
*From first day to last day,*
*Assembly ka one arm distance,*
*Without uniform - outline mai khade hona.*
*Birthday par toffees distribute karna.*
*Sabkuch best tha.*
*Exams ki cheating,*
*Teachers kai naye naye names rakhna,*
*Pta tha ki galt hai parr rakhte the names,*
*Har roj "gooooooddd moooorrrrrnnnnnniiiiggggg maaaaaaaammmmm",*
*Ka song sunnanna.*
*Vo school,*

*vo dost best the bus,*
*Penfight sai lekar thumbfight takk,*
*Kitni hi games hum picche baith kar khela karte the,*
*Chalk kai chhote chhote tukade, ek dusre ko marra karte the.*
*Agar ajj ek wish mil jaye,*
*Toh wish hogi ki school life dubara jenne ko mil jaye!....*

# 2. Purri school life

*Mushkil tha subha jaldi uthna or school jaana,*
*Kyunki karni padti thi vo cheez jo ham hate karte the.*
*Chhote hote toh friends sai bhi jealousy karte the,*
*Ghar par bhi padhna,*
*school mai bhi padhna,*
*Sabse kaam percentage class mai 95 jaate the,*
*1st_$2^{nd}$ mai itne obedient or sincere hote the,*
*Ajj soch kar bhi hassi aati hai !...*
*Abb ham bade ho rahe the aur yeh values,*
*kaam ho rhi thi.*
*Abb friends kai liye school jaate the,*
*Abb highest percentage hi 95 hoti thi,*
*Abb friends kai sath jealousy nhi hoti thi,*
*Balki agar unko punishment milti,*
*toh sath khud bhi khade ho jaate the.*
*Chhote hote test kai liye padh kar jaate the or bade hokar,*
*Test bina padhe, cheating kar kar hi dete the.*
*Kitna change aa gya tha!!...naa*
*Chhote hote jaise the, bade hokar purre opposite.*
*Class kai sath sath habits change hoti gyi aur friendship strong.*
*Abb $10^{th}$ aa gyi thi,*
*Bond strong bhot ho gya tha or abb tutne vala tha.*

*Parr ek cheez first or last day mai common thi,*
*Vo tha hamara unhappy hona!!...*

# 3. Pehla Din

*Zindagi ka pehla din toh kisi ko yaad nhi hota,*
*Arey! Hoga bhi kaise.*
*Par hamare dusre ghar "School" jaane ka pehla din halka halka yaad hai.*
*Jab mamma papa kai sath admission karvane gye the,*
*Principal ma'am nai toffee di thi lga tha,*
*school bhot accha hoga.*
*Abb admission ho gyi thi, uniform lene gye,*
*Shirt 18number ki jagahen 20 ki kyun?*
*Shoes 10number ki jagahen 11 ke kyun?*
*lene ka logic samajh nhi aaya tha.*
*Finally, school jaane ka din tha,*
*Naya bag pack karke, acchi tarah tyar hokar, bottle Galle mai latka kar school jaane ke time sai aada ghanta pehle tyaar the.*
*Mamma papa school chodne gye.*
*school kai aunty ko jab pakdaya,*
*toh aansu nikal gye,*
*aur maa ko bhi bechan kar diya tha.*
*Class mai mam nai pehle pyaar sai,*
*Phir draa kar or phir dantt kar chup karvane ki koshish ki parr ham nhi manne....*
*Saare pehle din roo kar hi aate hain,*

*Or jo roo kar nhi aate.*
*vo aagle din sai toh,*
*roo kar hi aate hain.*
*Pta nhi kaab tak yeh roona dhona chalaya.*
*Parr school jaana chhote hote kabhi nhi bhaya!!...*

# 4. School Bag

*15 saal (Arrey! Nursery to 12th )ki school life mai bhot kuch badal jaata hai,*
*Hamari habits, choices, preferances, shaunk aur bhi bhot kuch.*
*Hamare kitne hi school bag badal jaate hain,*
*Hamare school bag ki bhi naa ek journey hoti hai.*
*Primary classes mai har session ki starting mai naya bag hota tha,*
*Naya bag, nayi kit, nayi books or nayi class ka first day most favourite and awaited hota tha.*
*Parr yeh aadat bade hote hote badal gyi thi.*
*Abb naa nya bag lete the, naa nyi books,*
*3 saal purani Edition vali books seniors sai mill jaati thi.*
*Geometry, kit ka toh koi use hi nhi rha tha,*
*Abb bus bag mai ek pen hi mil jaye vo hi bhot hota tha.*
*Books ki bhi naa bag sath ek journey hoti thi.*
*Primary classes mai ratt ko bag pack karne mai 15 minute lagate the,*
*Har subject ki book, notebook or ek rought notebook lekar jaate the,*
*Teacher ki dantt ka darr jo tha.*
*Yeh Silsila kaab ek notebook yah khali bag par aa gya pta hi nhi chala,*

*Abb dusre section sai book laane mai time nhi lagta tha,*
*Or teachers ko bhi pta tha ki yeh inki book nhi hai.*
*Itni haad parr kar di thi ki,*
*Ki agar physics ki book na milti toh chemistry ki book khol lete the,*
*Geography ki jagah economics ki, Hindi kai period mai english ki,*
*Hamne toh sirf book hi show karni hoti thi.*
*Primary classes mai toh bag ka weight bhot jayada hota tha,*
*Or senior classes mai bag toh sirf show karne kai liye hi lekar jaate the.*
*Hamare school Bag ki journey 15 saal chali, Or uske bad, school life hi end ho gyi !!....*

# 5. School ki Dosti

*Sare log jo hamari zindagi mai aate hain,*
*Temporary hi toh hote hain.*
*Par school kai kayin dost permanent hote hain.*
*Section change ho jaate the,*
*Par dusri class mai ek dusre ko milne jaate the.*
*Bhagh kar aane-jaane mai toh ek Barr saans phul jaati thi*
*par hamari dosti kabhi kamzoor nhi hone di thi.*
*Nursery sai lekar 12$^{th}$ tak ham sath rahe.*
*Hum chahe kitne bhi talented, intelligent naa hoo,*
*Par ham dosto ki nazar mai bewakuf hi the.*
*Ek dusre ki insult karne mai Hum no.1 the,*
*Agar koi gussa mann jaata toh "teri izzat hai?" keh kar hassa dete the.*
*Ulta jawab dena hamari aadat thi,*
*Binna insult kiye toh batt hi nhi hoti thi,*
*Par ek dusre kai sath har time khadhte the.*
*Ek dusre ka tiffin chhura kar khana,*
*Ek ko punishment milti toh sath dusre nai bhi khad jaana.*
*Ek dusre ko apne secrets btana,*
*or phir "let me spill the beans" bool kar blackmail karna,*
*or apna kaam krvana.*
*Jab ek din friend school na aaye,*

*Toh aagle din picchle din ki saari kahaniyan btana,*
*Bhot accha lagta tha.*
*Abb school vale doston kai sath roj mulakat toh nhi hoti,*
*Par unka sath zarur hai sath.*
*Or jab bhi unko phone karo apni life sai tired hokar,*
*Dil halka ho jaata hai.*
*Orr jabb bhi call pai bat hoti hai naa, Pta nhi kyun?*
*Abb bhi, Apnapan saa mehsus hota hai!!....*

# 6. Annual Function

*Annual function ki bhot yaadein hain.*
*One month pehle sai tyaari aur hamari masti shuru ho jaati thi,*
*Last kai 3 periods miss karte the,*
*Annual function ki tayari kai first two days toh,*
*hum sare dances, skits, songs dekhte the.*
*or joo sabse accha lgta tha usme ho jaate the.*
*1month practice karke burra haal ho jaata tha.*
*Annual function sai ek do din pehle,*
*Jis din dresses milni hoti thi,*
*tab saare present hote the.*
*Annual function vale din 3 ghante pehle bulate the,*
*2 ghante toh tyaar hone mai hum nikal dete the,*
*Or ek ghanta bore hote the.*
*Annual function start hone sai pehle,*
*backstage sai parents aayen hai yahnhi dekhne jaate the.*
*Apni performance ka wait karte-karte,*
*Bag khali or tummy full kar lete the,*
*orr abb hum karr bhi kya saktein the?*
*Ek room mai band rehna for an hour or two was not at all easy for us.*
*Performance ki starting mai nervous hote the,*
*Or end tak saara kahana digest kar lete the.*

*Performance kai badd binna kapde badle refreshment lene bhagh jaate the,*
*Kapde badal kar aage ka function dekhne jaate the.*
*Uske badd kayin functions dekhe,*
*Parr apne school ka annual function hi best tha!...*

# 7. Assembly

*School ki harr cheez hi best thi,*
*School ki morning assembly bhi toh mastt thi.*
*Vaise kabhi kabhi morning assembly,*
*noon assembly bhi bann jaati thi,*
*Winter's main!*
*But assembly toh assembly hoti hai naa,*
*Vahin masti chahe subha kare yah dupher ko,*
*Masti toh masti thi naa.*
*Bell bajte hi class kai bahar line banna leni,*
*Nails bade hote toh teeth sai katt lete the,*
*Ribbons, Tie, Belt toh class mai ek extra rakhi hui thi.*
*Second Bell hote hi march-pass karte hue ground mai jaana,*
*Sath-sath aage vale friends kai shoes utarana, mast tha naa.*
*Ground mai one arm distance par khadna,*
*Picche khadne kai liye friends kai sath ladna,*
*Agar Ek improper uniform mai hota,*
*toh dusre nai tie yah belt uttar deni.*
*Orr uske sath outline mai chale jaana,*
*Kitna aacha tha naa.*
*Prayer mai ek aankh khol karr sabko dekhna,*
*Pledge, thought, word of the day yah news ki turn hoti thi,*
*Toh chhuti mar lete the.*

*Yah phir,*
*Sir dard ka bhana marr kar class mai bath jaate the.*
*National Anthem mai bilkul sidhe khade hote the,*
*Assembly kai badd march pass karte hue apni class ko Ravana hote the.*
*Abb toh sirf assembly ki yaadein hai sath,*
*Or sacchi mai lagta hai vo din bhi kya din the!!...*

# 8. School Trip

*5 day tour parr toh saare dost nhi jaa paate the,*
*Par one day trip parr sare jaate the.*
*Trip pai jaane sai ek din pehle toh nind nhi aati thi,*
*Pehle toh nind hi nhi aati thi,*
*Orr agar aa jaati toh uthne kai time sai ek ghanta pehle hi aankh khul jaati thi.*
*Bag cold-drink, fastfood sai bhara hota tha.*
*School bhi time sai pehle pahunch jaate the.*
*Bus mai friends kai sath window seat kai liye fight karte the.*
*Picnic spot par pahunch kar hooting karte the,*
*Jab counting or attendance ho rhi hoti thi vo time bhot boring time hota tha.*
*Apni destination par pahunch kar purri masti karne lagte the,*
*Buss kaami sirf phones ki hoti thi.*
*Ghar vapas aakar,*
*purri kahani ghar valo ko sunnate the.*
*Abb tak kayin trips par gye hain.*
*Family kai sath bhi or friends kai sath bhi,*
*Or abb phones bhi hote hain,*
*Parr vo majja,*
*Jo school kai dosto kai sath*
*School days mein aata tha naa,*

*vo majja hi nhi aata hai!!....*

# 9. Barish ka Din

*Arrey, kahani ka naam sun kar kiski yaad aagyi!*
*Par nhi, yeh uss barish kai din ki nhi, Us barish kai din ki batt hai,*
*Jab Monday ko, bahar kaale baadal hote or maa kehti beta ajj school matt jaa.*
*Arrey nhi maa,*
*Assesment hai yeh keh kar school bhagh jaana,*
*Window seat kai liye friends kai sath fight karna,*
*Chall jiski nasib mai thi usko mil jaati thi, Seat.*
*Challo koi batt nhi!*
*Science ka period mai, ma'am chemistry padha rhe the,*
*or ham sab bahar chaal rhi tej havao(winds) ko apni kahaniyan sunna rhe the.*
*Ma'am nai padhana band kardiya,*
*Ek nai kha mam padhao naa, tab dusro ko hosh aaya,*
*phir sorry bool - boolkar mam ko padhane ke liye manaya.*
*Parr issi waqat bell ho gyi,*
*Mam gye or saare nachne lag gye,*
*Timetable dekha,*
*Arrey, yeh toh Punjabi ka period hai,*
*Koi washroom kai bhane toh koi teacher sai kaam kai bahane,*
*Saare bahar school campus mai ghum rhe the,*

*Koi samosa kha rha tha toh koi bhature or koi hawa.*
*Jab sir class mai aaye toh sirf ginti kai paanch bacche the,*
*Phir kya tha, purra din hawa or barish sai apni batte ki,*
*parr class mai baith kar nhi,*
*stage par khade hokar.*
*Abb chhuti ki bell hui, sare bags le aaye,*
*Abb bottles toh paani ki bhari hui thi,*
*Ek nai cheekar mai jump kiya orr,*
*Dusre paanch ko bhigaya,*
*too dusro nai apni bottles sai usko nehlaya.*
*Abb pta nhi koi vahan hai,*
*toh koi kahan parr*
*Abb vo vaqt toh vapas nhi aa sakta,*
*Par baarish kai saath, un dosto ki yaad zarur aati hai!...*

# 10. Exams

*Exams:*

*Inki vajah sai toh school life perfect nhi hoti,*

*Varna school without exams toh kisi tourist place sai kaam nhi hota.*

*Pta nhi kisne exams ka panga daal diya, Or hame abb inko jhelnaa pad rha hai.*

*Har saal 4-4 barr exams dete the,*

*Or $9^{th}$, $10^{th}$, $11^{th}$, $12^{th}$ mai toh aangint barr exams hote the.*

*Exams toh school kai badd bhi chal rahe hain,*

*Parr school kai exams ki yaadein hi aalag hain.*

*Datesheet milte hi diary yah table par chipka lete the,*

*Exam sai ek din pehle 2-3 ginti kai bacche hi school jaate the.*

*Paper vale din:*

*School jạkar sabse pehle apni seat dhundhna.*

*First seat vale dukh manate the, Or last seat vale khush ho jaate the,*

*Uske badd examiner Koon hai vo dekhna.*

*Reading time mai M.C.O's ki cheating kar lete the yah krva dete the.*

*Forehead ko touch karte the toh dusra samajh jaata tha ‘A‘*

*Agar nose toh ‘B’*

*Agar mouth toh ‘C‘*

*Or agar chin toh 'D'*
*Agar TOD( Teacher on Duty) accha hota toh answer sheet tak change kar lete the.*
*Or agar nhi toh aankho sai answer bta dete the.*
*Washroom jaana toh har paper kai ritual hota tha,*
*Chahe paper complete hoye yah naa.*
*Par hamne washroom jaana hota tha.*
*Paper hone kai badd jo halla hota tha vo alag hi tha,*
*Marks ki discussion bhi mastt hoti thi.*
*Paper accha jaata toh,*
*Canteen par samose or cold-drink ki party hoti thi,*
*Agar naa jaye toh,*
*Sidha ghar ko ravana tolly hoti thi.*
*Vo school kai paper life kai papers sai toh easy the,*
*Kyunki ham sabb dost jo sath the!!...*

# 11. Result Day

*Bhagwan ka naam lete hue sote the, result sai ek din pehle.*
*Subah chehare ka raang uttara hota tha,*
*Dheere dheere school kai liye tyaar hote the,*
*Or parents kai sath school jaate the.*
*Class kai taraaf jaate time,*
*dil bhot teej dhadhak rha hota tha.*
*Itna daar toh injection lagavne time bhi nhi lagta jitna darr lag rha hota tha.*
*Result accha aata toh purra din khush rhte the,*
*friends ko call karke btate the.*
*Parr accha naa aata toh vahan hi danntt par jaati thi,*
*Orr Ghar aa kar toh burra haal ho jaata tha.*
*Or yeh haal saal mai chaar barr hota tha.*
*Par vo exams or result day,*
*Life kai exams or failures sai toh soo gunna acche the!!.....*

# 12. Recess

*4th period kai end ki bell jaise hi bajti thi,*
*Sare bacche eise bhagate the,*
*jaise jail sai 100 saal baad chhute ho.*
*Or bhagte bhi kyun naa?*
*Abb recess hai,*
*Or recess ki memories bhi bohot hain.*
*20 minutes ki recess mai khana khane mai toh sirf 5minute hi lagate the hum,*
*Kyunki aade tiffins toh recess sai pehle hi khaali hote the.*
*Bell hote hi ma'am ka sentence purra hone nhi dete the,*
*or bahar bhaag jaate the.*
*Pehle purre school kai 2 chakkar lagane,*
*dusre section or dusri classes ki khabaren jaanate the.*
*apne bestfriend kai sath long walk par jaane kai binna,*
*Hamari Recess purri kahan hoti thi.*
*Abb aati thi khana khaane ki barri,*
*Bacche hue tiffins pai saare toot padte the,*
*Tiffin mai maggi or sandwich ka toh najara hi alag hota tha.*
*Abb kuch khelne ki barri hoti thi.*
*Maths ki notebook ko bat or papers ki ball kai sath cricket khelte the.*
*Majja toh tab aata tha,*

*jab ball kisi ko lag jaati or batsman ko dantt padd rhi hoti thi.*
*Bohot Khushi hua karti thi jab bell late hua karti thi.*
*Yaad aayenge yeh din bohot kahan ham yeh soccha karte the,*
*Abb mangate hain buss yahin ki bus,*
*Ek-din,*
*sirf ek-din school life ka dubara jeene ko mil jaaye!!....*

# 13. Hamari Water Fight

*Kehte hai naa ek aadmi mai aneko gun hote hain,*
*Ek cheez aneeek kaam aati hai,*
*Jaise hamari waterbottles hi Lelo.*
*Yeh sirf paani leke jaane kai kaam nhi aati,*
*Balki inke sath toh aaneko yaadein juddi huin hain.*
*Papers mai bottle Dene kai bahane answer batana,*
*Ek bottle bharne ki permission mange toh,*
*dusro nai chilla-chilla kar kehna "meri bhi bottle leja."*
*Yeh toh chhoti chhoti masti bhari yaadein hai,*
*Meri toh favourite hoti thi, Ek dusre kai sath holi khelna, Holi?*
*Par holi or bottle ka relation kya Hua?*
*Arrey, purri batt toh suno,*
*Paani vali Holi khelna,*
*Rojj, hamari Holi hoti thi.*
*Roj kisi na kisi ko target banana or usko Ghar nehlakar bhejhna.*
*Ek Barr toh hadd hi hogyi,*
*Maine prank kiya ,*
*Dost class sai bahar gyi hui thi,*
*ma'am abhi aaye nhi the.*
*Uski seat par paani ghira diya,*
*Or jab vo aayi,*

*Usko batto mai uljha kar seat par bitha diya.*
*Or phir kya tha,*
*Uske reaction sai pehle, ham sare lastbenchers ki hassi nikal gyi.*
*Uska toh reaction dekhne vala tha,*
*Abhi ma'am nhi aaye the,*
*Phir kya tha,*
*Buss bottle uthai orr main bhaghi or meri picche vo,*
*Samne sai sir aagye,*
*wish karkar side sai nikalgye,*
*Class mai jabb school ghum kar vapas aana hua,*
*Toh 3 jaano nai ikhate paani daala.*
*Challo, koi batt nhi,*
*Seat pai baith gye.*
*Class mai mam aagye Parr hamare gooooodddd*
*affftttteeeerrrrnoooonnnnnn vale song ka reply nhi diya,*
*Or sidha lecture sunaya,*
*Is wing ki sabse senior class ki halat dekho,*
*Hamne kha, mam class saf krdi.*
*Hadd, toh tabb hogyi, Jab chhuti time,*
*gate tak jaate hue maine uspe sara water bottle ka paani daal diya,*
*Or sir nai dekh liya,*
*Or principal pass le gye.*
*Principal mam nai kha "ese kon karta hai?"*
*Muh sai nikal gya "Hum",*
*Mam nai ghura or warning letter issue kardi.*
*Ek baarr toh mini heart attack aagya tha.*

*par abb lgta hai,*
*Ki vo warning letter bhi kitni acchi thi naa.*
*Abb bhi waterbottle payas toh bhujhati hai parr un dino ki yaad bhi dilla deti hai,*
*Or chehere par ek baddi si muskan la deti hai!....*

# 14. Priceless Moment

*School masti kai sath sath kayin priceless moments ka ghar bhi tha.*
*Jab school ko state, command level pai aapne represent karna hota tha,*
*Toh vo bhot zimadari vala kaam lgta tha.*
*Chahe sports mai, chahe quiz mai or chahe debate main,*
*Mehnat toh bohot karte the, Teachers bhi or ham bhi,*
*Chhuti kai badd school mai rukna, subah jaldi uthna, ratt ko derr sai Sona,*
*Bohot mehnat karte the.*
*Competition vale din,*
*Principal, teachers aur students ki expectations hoti thi.*
*Aur stomach mai butterflies,*
*Jaise-teise apna best dete the,*
*Or jab result aana hota tha,*
*Tab aankhe band hoti thi or fingers crossed.*
*Agar position naa aati toh ek Barr disappoint toh ho jaate the,*
*Par teachers honsla badha dete the.*
*Orr jabb position aati toh Khushi sai aansu aajaate the,*
*Teachers sai appreciation milna,*
*baddi si smile laa deta tha,*
*Aabhi toh Ghar aake friends or family sath party hoti thi,*

*Orr jaab relatives ko phone hota tha ki*
*hamara baccha national level mai $2^{nd}$ aaya hai,*
*Toh sacchi bhot accha lagta tha.*
*Jis din stage par announce hota tha, trophies milti thi,*
*vo din bohot khaas hota tha.*
*If I would have to choose between Goa trip and result moment,*
*I would have surely choosen to relive vo result vala din.*
*Wo buss priceless tha!!....*

# 15. Birthday ki Yaadein

*Birthday sabka favourite or most awaited day hota hai,*
*Birthday party, wishes, gifts ka wait hota hai.*
*School toffees, chocolates leke jaane ki tyaari do din pehle sai hi shuru ho jati thi,*
*School jakar friends wish badd mai karte the pehle chocolates mangte the.*
*1st period mai toffees bantne 3_4 dosto ko lekar nikal jaate the,*
*Purra din lgta tha hame toffees distribute karne kai liye.*
*Chhote hote classmates ko ek,*
*friends ko doo*
*or bestfriend ko ten toffees dete the.*
*Parr badde hokar,*
*Purri class handfull of chocolates uthati thi.*
*Recess mai toh canteen par party pakki hoti thi,*
*Or shaam ko vaise party hoti thi.*
*Friends, Spray, Coke, sauce sai burra haal kardete the,*
*Or Nye kapde kharab kar dete the.*
*Birthday toh harr saal aata hai,*
*Par voo school mai unn dosto kai sath manaya hua Birthdays hi best the!!...*

# 16. Games period

*Sabse jayada Khushi tab hoti thi,*
*jaab Maths, Science ka period,*
*Games period mai badal jaata tha.*
*Or sabse jyada dukh tabb hota tha jab games period,*
*Maths, Science kai period mai badal jaata tha.*
*Games period mai majja tabb bhot aata tha jab purri class ikhate khelti thi.*
*Vo bhi bacchon vali game,*
*Choor-police, pakadan-pakdai etc. etc.*
*Or jabb koi slip ho jaata tha toh majak bohot banate the.*
*Hamari favourite game hamne hi invent ki thi,*
*Required material was water bottles, ball and ground ki mitti.*
*Just after reaching we started our waterfight,*
*Mitti ki holi or ball kai sath dusro ki pitai,*
*It sounds weird but Hum yahin kehlte the.*
*Purra period yahin karte the,*
*Kabhi - kabhi toh shirt kai ander mitti aur phir paani daal dete the.*
*You can very well imagine uska haal,*
*Ground sai class tak jaate time,*
*Apne hath dusro ki shirts sai saaf kar lete the.*
*Or raaste main har teacher yahin kehta,*

*Are you an English Medium School student?Don't seem like that.*
*Insult toh hoti thi par hamari konsa respect thi,*
*Or hamari masti sabse zaruri thi.*
*Abb yaad aate hain vo din,*
*Vo gandi uniform, vo mamma ki dantt,*
*Or school kai vo sare paal…or lagta hai vo din bhi kitne acche the!...*

# 17. School mai Pizza

*School mai Pizza toh thanda ho jaata tha, Naa hi cheese pull aata tha,*
*Parr yeh thanda pizza khaane ka mjja bohot aata tha.*
*Hua kya,*
*Ek din meri dost school mai Pizza lai.*
*Us ko recess mai bag mai dikha hi nhi, Lga ki ghar par rh gya,*
*Usne dusro ka khaana kha liya.*
*Abb 5th period mai book nikalte time pizza dikh gya,*
*Vo bhi 2 daabe the,*
*Hame dikhane lag gyi,*
*Abb period over ho gya,*
*Ma'am abhi Gaye nhi the ki,*
*haam uski seat par Jaa pahunche the.*
*Ek_doo nai usko pakda,*
*aur dusro nai pizza nikala,*
*toppings sari box kai sath lag gyi thi.*
*Parr, Ham sabne pizza base aur sause kai bhot majje uthaye.*
*Orr mam aagye,*
*Haan!pizza khatam kar liya tha.*
*Parr ek daaba pda tha,*
*period main pizza bringer washroom gya,*
*toh hamne pizza apne bag mai daal liya,*

*Vo bhi smart thi,*
*Aate hi......bag check kiya,*
*pizza nhi tha, toh sidha mam ko bool diya.*
*Uski insult hogyi par usko pizza mil gya.*
*Jab period over hua,*
*mam warn karke gye ki koi iske bag ko touch nhi karega.*
*Mam gye,*
*orr abb pizza box.... pizza bringer kai pass tha,*
*Chair par chad gyi, Ek slice toh loota gya,*
*Or dusra uske hath sai maine cheen liya,*
*Tha toh base aur sauce hi but yummy tha,*
*Or abb chhuti ho gyi thi, Taste kharab ho gya tha,*
*Toh canteen sai colddrink le kar pi thi.*
*Abb pizza toh garam-garam hota hai*
*or*
*cheese pull bhi accha aata hai,*
*Parr vo dosto kai sath,*
*school mai khaaye jaane vala pizza base hi best hota tha!.*

# 19. Fairwell Party

*School mai ajj hamara last function tha,*
*Nayi dresses main acchi tarah tyaar hokar,*
*pics click karva karr aaye the,*
*Abb hamara last function jo tha school main,*
*School mai aaka apna ritual purra kiya,*
*ek dusre ki insult karne ka.*
*Party shuru hui,*
*Tags bhi Mille,*
*Parr fairwell par rone dhone vale kaam hamne nhi kiye,*
*Par sabke dil ko kuch ho rha tha.*
*Par ham ek dusre ki insult karne par lage hue the.*
*Ek nai keh hi diya,*
*Kya hai hame kyun alag hona pad raha hai,*
*Par phir sabko lga,*
*Yeh din toh sabki life mai aaya tha or aaye gaa,*
*Dukhi kyun hona,*
*Hass kar jeete hain bacche hue din ek sath,*
*Aur yaadein bnate hain last exams takk.*
*Abb vakt ko toh koi rokk nhi skta.*
*Phir gate tak jaate time,*
*Songs sing karte hue gye,*
*teachers kai sath.*

*Or dil ko delasa dete hue,*

*Ki yeh toh hona hi tha.*

*Or abb aage vali life ko hass kar galle lagate hain!!....*

# 20. Last exam of 10th

*Ajj 10th class ka last exam tha.*
*Exam kai badd,*
*Apne school mai saare friends nai milne ka decide Kiya tha.*
*Har class mai Gaye, Sare teachers ki blessings li,*
*Pehli barr principal mam ki battein dhyan sai sunni thi.*
*Lag raha tha kuch bda nhi badlega but aandar sai feeling aa rhi thi ki sabkuch badal jayega.*
*Ek taraf excitement hai apne aage ki life ki, Or ek taraf sirf mayusi hai,*
*Kuch samajh hi nhi aa rha.*
*Apni class, apne playground mai vo lamhe dubara jeene ko nhi milenge,*
*Bus unki yaadein rahengi sath.*
*Par ham karr bhi kya saktein hain.*
*Last time canteen jaa kar samose khaye.*
*Playground mai gye, bench par bath kar,*
*Ek dusre ki leg pulling ki jaise karte the,*
*Mitti ek dusre kai uppar daali par paani nhi daala ajj,*
*Kyunki abhi shirts ko rangna bakki tha.*
*Apne - Apne sketches nikale aur shirts par,*
*chedne(Nick names), or apni insta and snapchat I'd likhi.*
*Promise Kiya tha,*

*Ki sabko yaad rakhenge par sabko pta thi ki sirf contact list mai save rahenge.*
*Abb bus chall pade saare sath, Or mudte gye apni apni raah par.*

# Part 2 : 3 Lessons

"*Update yourself before the world out dates you*"

-Zishan Ashraf

So, learn. Learn from every moment, every task.

I had drafted my sonnets, altered them as well. However, at some point. I asked myself, "What am I providing for my perusers?" Just pleasure of reading and enjoying sonnets.

Then, at that point, I considered composing the lessons which I learned while composing this book. Here, I have momentarily talked about three significant lessons which I learned while composing this book.

# 21. Self Doubting

*<u>Self Doubting - Age doesn't matter:</u>*

*"Age is no barrier. It's a limitation you put on your mind."*

*- Jackie Joyner Kersee*

*At the point when I first time I composed sonnets and from there on I chose to get them published. I self-questioned myself. Pondered the thought for a couple of days.*

*In the interim, I have not chosen. I went over instances of KFC Founder, J.K Rowling, and PrabhSimrat Gill in recordings and books. KFC Founder "Colonel Harland" began KFC at 66. J.K Rowling composed his overall blockbuster series of "Harry Potter" at 25. PrabhSimrat Gill creator of "Explore: The New You" hit bestseller at 14. Nadia Comaneci made her Olympics debut at 14.*

*Law of Attraction worked and I found the solution to my question that "Age doesn't make any difference whatsoever". We simply*

*self-question ourselves in view of some futile rationale. We ought to never do that. You really want to have those abilities, a passionate longing to accomplish something and you can do that. We have self-uncertainty in ourselves due to the disappointments, we confronted prior.*

*Somebody wise has said, "Failure is not the opposite of success, it is a part of Success." We all are extraordinary; we have our assets and shortcomings. We ought not to contrast ourselves as well as other people and quit questioning our abilities and would anything we like to do at whatever stage in life.Remember:*

*"The worst enemy to Creativity is Self-Doubt."*

*-Sylvia Plath*

# 22. Comfort Zone

*<u>You have to leave your comfort zone toachieve something.</u>*

*"A Comfort Zone is a beautiful place, but nothing ever grows there."*

*-John Assaraf*

*Yes, you have to leave your comfort zone. You are not even entering into your growth zone if you are living in your comfort zone.*

*All people dream of doing something great, but only 1% of people can achieve it. Let me tell you, why?*

*You must have heard this famous quotation of Vince Lombardi, "Winners don't quit, and quitters never win."*

*half of the individuals quit while they are in their usual range of familiarity. They do a tad of difficult work when they have the inspiration. Nonetheless, they rest for 8-10*

*hours, have food on schedule, do parties, scroll online media, sit around, and fall flat. And afterward, they say karma was not on their side and stopped.*

*Presently, there are extra half of individuals in the race. Yet, here the inquiry emerges why 49% of individuals quit?*

*Simply leaving your usual range of familiarity isn't sufficient. You run over many battles and numerous things you need to forfeit. You need to confront mental and passionate breakdowns and in the meantime, 40% more individuals quit. Presently, there are only 10% of individuals in the race, and just 1% of individuals succeed on the grounds that they can acknowledge their disappointments and demands brought to them by their predetermination. By then, they have battled a ton and are burnt out on the excursion such a lot of that, they quit effectively when they face any more battle,*

*penance, or run over a test of nature like genuine medical problems, passing of adored ones, and the sky is the limit from there.*

*1% of individuals who face all challenges, never stopped are achievers.*

*You need to leave your usual range of familiarity, battle, penance a ton of things, face disappointments and difficulties to see your fantasies turning into a reality.*

*Remember:*

*"The comfort zone is nothing else but a graveyard for your dreams and ideas"*

*-Anonymous*

# 23. Accepting Your Flaws

*Accepting your failures and learning fromthem :*

*"Accepting your failures helps you to not be a failure."*

*-Sameeksha*

*Yes, we should accept our failures. Generally, what we do is if we succeed, we take all the credits and if we fail, we make excuses like: I was not well, my team member was not good, and more and more. But it is wrong; we should accept our failures and learn from them. If your team member was not good, then you had to take action against him/her. Action is the key. You can't blame anyone for your failures. You failed because you didn't take the right action at the right time. And there is no use in regretting after you have failed.*

*It was your fault at all.*

*"Regret is useless in life. It's in the past. All we have is Now."*

*-Marlon Brando*

*Along these lines, you need to acknowledge your disappointments, gain from them, and never rehash them. Furthermore tolerating disappointments and attempting again isn't sufficient. Acknowledge your disappointments, above all, learn, distinguish the errors you did, where you needed, gain from them, and afterward attempt once more.*

*We want to gain from our disappointments additionally from others' disappointments as well. How often you will get come up short, learn and attempt once more?*

*To lessen this number, begin gaining from others' errors as well. Gain from them and don't rehash them.*

*"Life is too short to be learning from your mistakes. So, learn from others' too"*

*-Anonymous*

# About The Author

***Sameeksha Juneja*** was born and brought up in an Indian middle-class Family living in Fazilka, Punjab. She is currently a class9 (2021-22) student studying in Army Public School, Fazilka. Lockdown has been a life- changing period of her life. She built the habit of learning, reading books, attending workshops and seminars. She has been a National Level debator too. Besides this, she loves Maths, Economics, Chocolates, and getting her pictures clicked. She is serious about her life goals and visualizes herself as a Charted Accountant by 2029.

Now, let's see what destiny has intended her to be.

Thank you for showing your interest in this book. I hope you liked and enjoyed the poems.

Leave your reviews / thoughts / comments if any on @mastertowin at instagram. Tag this page or dm on this page.

I would love to hear from you!

9 798886 296228

Printed by Libri Plureos GmbH in Hamburg, Germany